I0580762

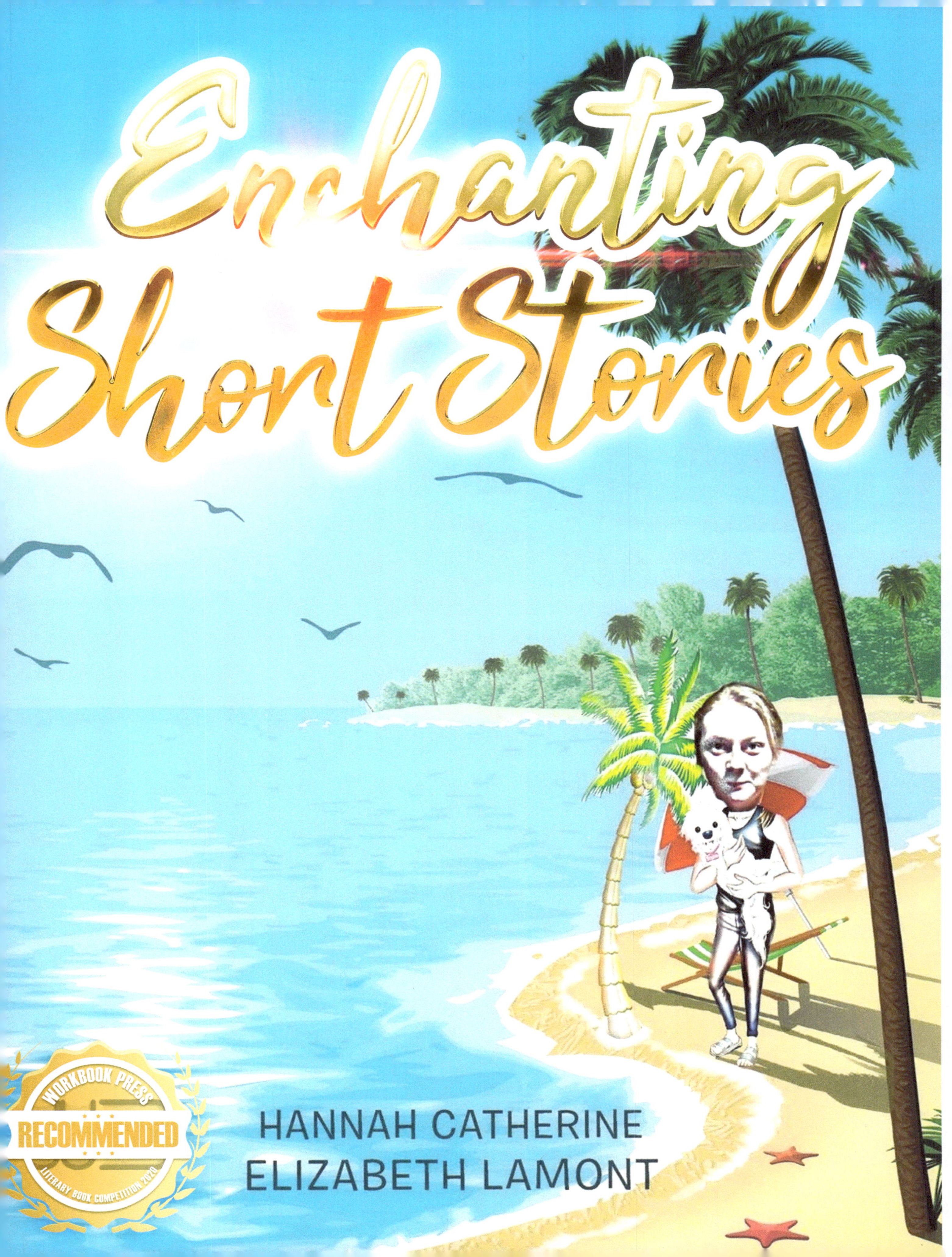

Enchanting
Short Stories
HANNAH CATHERINE
ELIZABETH LAMONT
WORKBOOK PRESS
RECOMMENDED
LITERARY BOOK COMPETITION 2020

WORKBOOK PRESS LLC
187 E Warm Springs Rd,
Suite B285, Las Vegas, NV 89119, USA

Website: https://workbookpress.com/
Hotline: 1-888-818-4856
Email: admin@workbookpress.com

Ordering Information:
Quantity sales. Special discounts are available on quantity purchases by corporations, associations, and others.
For details, contact the publisher at the address above.

ISBN-13:   978-1-956876-49-9 (Paperback Version)
                  978-1-956876-50-5 (Digital Version)

REV. DATE: 29/11/2021

Enchanting Short Stories

HANNAH CATHERINE
ELIZABETH LAMONT

Enchanting Short Stories

Hannah Catherine Elizabeth Lamont

The Brave Knight and the Duchess

Once upon a time, there was a kind-hearted duchess and a handsome, brave knight. He was the kindest in the land. One day as he was riding on his trusty white horse, he heard the most beautiful sound he could ever imagine, even in his wildest dreams. The knight followed the sound and came to an enchanted garden. And there was the loveliest young woman he had ever seen. He went up to her and introduced himself. 'Hello. My name is Aston. I am a knight.'

The woman replied, 'I am Isabella. I am the duchess of the enchanted garden and in charge of the garden and all the animals.' They talked for hours, and before they knew it, it was late and time to go home. So they said goodnight, and as they parted, they arranged to meet at the enchanted garden in the early morning.

Morning came, and as they agreed, they met up. They did this for a week, getting to know each other better. And after a week passed, they had started to fall madly in love.

Unknown to the young couple, an evil warlock had been watching them. The warlock wanted to marry Isabella because he wanted to become a duke and rule the enchanted garden. He had asked her to marry him before, but she refused him. He had seemed to disappear for a while, until one night he returned to the enchanted forest to ask her again. But he saw that she loved another.

Determined to marry her and become a duke, the warlock devised a plan. One night as the duchess slept in her enchanted garden, he crept up behind the duchess and grabbed her. Then he carried her off on his griffin to his cottage.

When the duchess awoke, she found herself in a scary, creepy cell. When the evil warlock came to ask her to marry him again, she replied, 'No. I don't care how many times you ask, it's still no.' The warlock just turned around and slammed and locked the door.

Later that day, Aston came to the enchanted garden for the duchess, but she was not there. When found her shawl on the ground, he knew that something was wrong. He quickly got on his horse and rode off to find the woman he loved. But before he left, he heard a sound. It was a one of the parrots Isabella looked after. The parrot told him what he saw. He told him about the warlock who took Isabella. The parrot told Aston he knew where the warlock lived would take him to her.

Meanwhile, back at his cottage, the warlock was planning on how to persuade the duchess to marry him. But in her cell, Isabella was thinking about her love for Aston, wondering, *Will Aston ever find me?*

A few days passed, and the evil warlock kept asking the duchess to marry him. And she still refused. After yet another failed attempt, the warlock stormed out of the cell and locked the door behind him.

Then Isabella heard a sound outside the cottage. It was a horse, so she looked outside the window and saw her brave knight. When she realised that he found her, she started singing to get his attention. When Aston heard the beautiful voice, he turned and saw her at the window. He came up to the window, and they talked for some time.

Then suddenly, the warlock crept up behind Aston, grabbed him, and brought him into the cottage. He opened the cell and told Isabella, 'If you do not marry me, I will destroy Aston.'

Aston begged her not to, but Isabella had no choice. She loved her brave knight so much, she agreed to marry the warlock. The warlock let Isabella out of the cell and put Aston inside.

The parrot saw what was going on and went to get help. Back at the warlock's cottage, the wedding of Isabella to the warlock was beginning. Poor Aston pacing back and forth, trying to figure out how to save his true love from this terrible fate.

Suddenly, he heard a sound coming from the cell window. It was the parrot with the keys to the door. Aston grabbed the keys. He looked out the window and saw that the parrot had brought all the animals. Aston devised a plan to free duchess. Aston would challenge the warlock, and while he kept the warlock busy, the animals would save Isabella.

When they found Isabella and the warlock, Aston challenged the warlock, and the animals saved his love. Aston and his opponent fought hard. Just as the warlock was about to kill him, Aston turned the table and destroyed the warlock.

Now free, the duchess ran towards Aston, who took the duchess upon his horse. and the knight and the duchess returned to the enchanted garden. Aston built a lovely cottage, and he, Isabella, and all the animals lived happily ever after.

The End

The Mermaid and the Princess

Once upon a time, there was a young princess named Dakota. She was very sad and lonely as she wanted more than to be stuck in the castle. She wanted more freedom, not on the land, but in the sea. She had dreamed of this since she was five years old. Dakota is sixteen now but still dreams of living in the sea.

One day she went riding on the beach. Dakota suddenly stopped when she saw what she thought was a mermaid. Excitedly, she rode back to her castle to tell her mother and her father. When she told them, they got very upset and sent her to her room. But she knew what she saw.

Later that night, she went back to where she saw the mermaid, but when she got there, there was no mermaid. As Dakota turned her horse to return home, she heard a splash. She looked around and saw the mermaid swimming towards her. Dakota asked her, 'What is your name?'

The mermaid replied, 'My name is Serena.' Dakota and Serena talked for what seemed like ages. Dakota told Serena that she wanted to be like her, so Serena asked, 'How about we switch places.'

Dakota thought about it for a wee while. She realised it might work as they looked so much alike. She agreed! So for months after that, Dakota went back to the ocean to teach Serena everything she needed to know about being a princess, her family, and herself. Serena did the same.

During that time, Serena learned that mermaids could turn human for one month. The next time Serena and Dakota met, they switched places. Serena became human, and Dakota became a mermaid. Dakota said, 'Remember, we swap back in a week.'

'What time?' Serena asked.

'What about noon?' With that settled, Dakota and Serena parted to start their new week-long adventure. Dakota went to meet Serena's family and friends, and Serena, in turn, did the same.

When Serena got to the castle, her first thought was to meet Dakota's parents. After spending the afternoon with them, she felt a strange connection to Dakota's father and mother. The next morning, Serena decided to spend the day learning about those lovely people and the land where they lived.

In the sea, Dakota was having a wonderful time, meeting all the different creatures and the enjoying the sights of the sea. She was so happy and loved life in the sea. She was beginning to wonder if she could ever go home as she felt as if something was missing.

All too soon, the week was over. And as they had agreed, Dakota and Serena met at the beach. But they decided to spend another week living each other's life.

Halfway through the second week, Dakota's father and mother asked to speak to Serena, as they had something very important to discuss with her. Serena was worried because she thought Dakota's parents had found out who she was.

But when the king opened his mouth, all that came out was, 'You have a sister.' She was shocked, so shocked that she started speaking a weird language. When the king tried to calm her down, he asked, 'Dakota, were you speaking dolphin?'

Serena asked, 'How do you know how dolphins speak?'

The king put his arm around her, sat her down, and told the truth. 'Long before I met your mother, I lived in the sea. I was a merman, but I felt trapped in the sea. I never told anyone. Then a wonderful thing happened. I met your mother and fell deeply in love with her. Then I asked the sea sorcerer if I could become human. He said "Yes, but if you get her to fall in love with you in three days, you have to give me your child when you're married." At the time, I didn't think about it. I was not sure if your mother would have me, so I said yes. The sea sorcerer turned me into a human, and your mother and I fell madly in love with each other. A year later, we got married and had two lovely daughters. By this time, I had forgotten the deal I made with the sea sorcerer. Then one day you and your sister were playing in the sea, and the sea sorcerer took your sister. We never saw her again. And that's why we don't let you near the sea.'

'What's her name?'

The queen answered, 'Her name's Serena.'

Then she spoke up. 'I'm Serena!'

The king and queen looked at each other, shocked. Serena started to explain, but they decided go to the sea and get Dakota.

Reunited, they explained everything to Dakota, and she was so very happy. Dakota asked how Serena escaped the sea sorcerer, and Serena answered, 'He died when I was six. Since then, I've been living with a group of very nice mermaids.'

The king and queen decided to move near the sea, much to the princess' delight. Serena and Dakota were able to swim in the sea as much as they wanted and go home to their parents at night. Everyone was so happy.

The End

The Magic Box

My name is Annie, and this is how my adventure began.

I met my two best friends, Lisa and Dominique, at high school. They were the funniest, nicest people I had ever met.

Anyway, it was near the end of summer holidays, and we decided to go camping in the nearby forest. When we got there, we set up camp, got something to eat, and then decided to go for a walk.

After a while, we came across a scary-looking old house. We went inside and saw a creaky, old staircase and decided to have a look upstairs. We went into the room at the top, and I tripped over a dusty old box on the floor. We tried to open it, but without success. We picked up the box, and underneath it was a note. It said, 'This magic box belonged to Sebastian the warlock, and the key should be nearby.'

We looked around the house and then tried outside. I looked amongst some wild flowers and found a rusty old key. I called to Dominique and Lisa, 'I think I found it!'

We went back upstairs to see if the key would fit. And to our surprise, it did. We held our collective breaths and started to turn the key. But to our disappointment, it did not turn as the key was too old and rusty. We decided to take the box back to camp.

Back at camp, we made dinner. Then Lisa turned in for the night. Dominique and I could not sleep because we were far too excited about the box. We talked about what could be in the box.

While we were talking, we suddenly heard a worrying sound coming from Lisa's tent. It was Lisa, crying. We asked her what was wrong, and she said that she wanted to go home. I suggested that we since we had a big day and a big adventure, maybe we should pack up all our things, including the box, and go home.

As it wasn't that late, we stopped off at Lisa's house and explained to her mum. Dominique and I told Lisa that we'd see her tomorrow. I asked who would take the box, and Dominique told me I should take it. I said that was okay, and off we went home.

The next morning, we went back to school. As I put things in my locker, I heard someone say, 'Hello.' I closed the door and saw a girl. I said hello back, and she told me that her name was Rachel and was new at school, so I welcomed her.

And then I noticed her necklace. It was exactly the same as the one we found at the old house. When I asked her about it, she told me, 'My dad left it to me. It's supposed to open a box, but I have looked everywhere in my house and couldn't find it then.'

I explained everything to her about the house and the box, and that I had taken it home with me. When the bell rang, I asked Rachel if she could meet me and my friends after school, and she agreed.

Before we knew it, school was over. I saw Dominique and Lisa, and I told them everything Rachel had said about the box, and that she was meeting up with us.

When Rachel joined us, I suggested that we go to my house since that's where the box was. When we got their, we went up to my room and got the box out from under my bed. Rachel, Dominique, Lisa, and I were so excited. We just sat there, wondering what could be in the box. Rachel said clothes, Lisa said shoes, Dominique said make-up, and I said books.

Rachel took her key from around her neck and opened the box. To our disappointment, there was nothing in the box but a note saying that it was a magic box. According to the note, all you had to do was put your hand over the box, and it would give you what you wished for.

We decided that Rachel should have the first wish since it was her box. She told us that she always wanted to go to Disneyland, so we put our hands over the box and wished. And and before we knew it, we were in Disneyland! We were so amazed. We walked around, and after we had our adventure, we wondered how we would get home. I tried saying, 'Home,' and to our amazement, it worked. We were home, and we still had the box. And we wanted to talk about what to do about the rest of the wishes. But it was getting late, and everyone had to get home. We made a plan to meet up at the old house to talk about it. Dominique, Lisa, and I decided that Rachel should take the box as it was hers to begin with.

Before we knew it, it was morning. We went to the old house decided to have a look around. We split up and searched for clues about the box.

Then all of a sudden, I heard a crash. I rushed in the direction of the sound to see what happened. It was Rachel! She had caught her foot on the bottom of the wardrobe. I asked if she was okay, and she said yes. As she picked herself up, she noticed a satchel inside the wardrobe. And inside the satchel was a journal.

We looked through the journal and discovered it was about the box. It told how it worked and how long the magic worked. Then suddenly, it ended.

So we decided to leave. Rachel took the journal, and we went to her house to decide what we should do. Lisa said that we should all go on grand adventures together. We all agreed it was a fantastic idea.

After a few days went, we decided to take another adventure. So after school, we went to Rachel's house to get the box and wished to go on an adventure, but it did not work. We figured out that the wishes were done. But we were not sad as we had lots of fun times and memories. Rachel kept everything her dad left her, including the box. I said, 'Even though the box does not work anymore does not mean that we can't do our own adventures.'

We were all excited. Rachel said, 'We have to come up with a cool nickname.'

Lisa suggested, 'How about the Adventure Squad?' We all agreed it was awesome. And it was off to star our own adventures together. The most perfect thing we got out of all the wishes was the best of friendships.

The End

The Prince and Princess of India

A very long time ago, a beautiful princess named Zeta lived in a mystical land known as India. She was married to the handsome Prince Rama, who was banished to the enchanted forest by his jealous stepmother, Queen Kika.

One day Princess Zeta saw a wounded deer in woods and begged Rama to help it. Rama drew a circle on the ground and said, 'This is a magic circle. As long as you stay in it, no harm will come to you.'

That night, the princess heard a horrible cry, 'Ah, help!' Thinking it was her beloved Rama in danger, Zeta ran from the circle.

She soon came across an old beggar man. Although Zeta had no money to give him, she could not refuse his plea and gave him one of her bracelets. As soon as he had the bracelet, the man turned into the ten-headed demon Revona. He grabbed the princess and took her to his castle, intending to make her his bride. The evil Revona locked her in the tower, and there she stayed for weeks, just looking out of the window and missing her dear Prince Rama terribly.

Rama approached the thorny palace unaware that Revona was watching him. The evil Revona was not through yet. He took a bow that could hold not one but ten arrows, each filled with a deadly poison. The arrows sped through the air, heading straight for Rama. The arrows hit the ground, releasing a poisonous thick yellow smoke.

As the smoke from Revona's arrows began to lift, a wonderful thing happened. A gazelle lay down next to Rama, sacrificing his life for Prince Rama's. When Rama came back to life, he raced to the monster's castle to rescue Zeta. Just then, Revona appeared. Rama shot an arrow into the sky, creating thunder, and destroyed Revona.

Princess Zeta ran down the stairs into Rama's arms. They went back to the enchanted forest, where they lived happily ever after.

The End

Rachel's Story

Hi. The story I am going to tell you is about a young girl named Rachel. Now you're probably wondering why I am telling you this. Well I'll tell you why. Because it shows us no matter what people say, always follow your dreams.

Rachel came from downtown Brooklyn. She graduated from college and became a part-time hairdresser. Though she enjoyed it, being a hairdresser was not what she wanted to do. She had a dream, and her dream was to be like her heroine, Selena Gomez. Yes, she wanted to become a singer.

Rachel tried everything. After work she went out to see if anyone needed a singer but had no luck. But did she stop there? Oh no. Rachel knew if she kept her dream and her heart open, something would come up.

Then one day something did come up. Rachel was at work, during her tea break, she turned on the radio, and Selena Gomez came on, and it was her favourite round and round. Then Rachel started singing. She imaged herself onstage and a big crowed shouting, 'Rachel', over and over again after she sang.

But then realised it was only her boss, Mr Jackson. 'Sorry, Mr Jackson, I was just singing.'

'I know. You were supposed to be working. Your tea break ended an hour ago. If you're through singing, there's a costumer waiting.'

Rachel went to the costumer and asked if she could help him. He answered, 'No, but can I help you.' He explained that he was looking for a talented singer. 'And I think I found one.' He also explained that he was walking by, heard her singing, and thought that she was good. He wanted to hear more. He gave Rachel his card and said, 'Have a think about it, and come by at that address.'

She thought about it, and the next day, she went to the address and said that she was looking for Mr Benson, and he called her over. He asked her name and age She said her name was Rachel and that she was nineteen. He told her to get up on the stage and sing something. Rachel asked, 'What shall I sing?' He said she could sing anything anything she wanted. So she sang "Who Says?" by Selena Gomez.

When Rachel finished the song, Mr Benson said that she was good. She was so good that he gave her a chance to do a Hollywood Broadway competition in just two weeks!

Rachel was so nervous all she did was practice. Before she knew it, the day came, and she was realising her dream. When her name came up, the announcer said, 'Please welcome Rachel.' She took a big breath and then sang another Selena Gomez song, "It's Magic." When she finished her song, she got what she wanted. She had won the Hollywood Broadway competition.

Well, that was basically it. Rachel had done it; she lived her dream. She still does lots of shows everywhere. But she also became a music teacher to help and teach kids to follow their dreams because no matter what people say, always follow your dream.

You're probably wondering who is telling this story. Maybe I should tell you my name is Rachel. I'm the singer and the music teacher.

The End

www.ingramcontent.com/pod-product-compliance
Lightning Source LLC
Chambersburg PA
CBHW041923180726
48295CB00002B/60